FUN FIRST CONCEPTS

LET'S LEARN SHAPES

by Anna C. Peterson

W9-DBA-788

TABLE OF CONTENTS

tadpole
books

WORDS TO KNOW

circle

diamond

octagon

rectangle

square

triangle

LET'S LEARN SHAPES!

sign

I see a circle.

I see a square.

deer

I see a triangle.

I see a diamond.

I see a rectangle.

car

I see an octagon.

LET'S REVIEW!

What shapes do you see below?

INDEX

FUN FIRST CONCEPTS

What color is a ladybug? What letters do your favorite items start with? Learn to count and recognize colors, shapes, and letters around you with these fun books! Have you read them all?

F&P Text Level Gradient™
Officially Leveled by **Fountas & Pinnell**

LOOK FOR OTHER TITLES IN THE SERIES:

FUN FIRST CONCEPTS
LET'S LEARN COLORS
tadpole books

FUN FIRST CONCEPTS
LET'S LEARN COUNTING
tadpole books

FUN FIRST CONCEPTS
LET'S LEARN LETTERS
tadpole books

FUN FIRST CONCEPTS
LET'S LEARN SHAPES
tadpole books

jump!

www.jumplibrary.com
www.jumplibrary.com/teachers

IL: Grades PreK–1

ISBN 978-1-64527-321-9

9 781645 273219

I SEE TREES

tadpole
books

TOOLS FOR TEACHERS

- **ATOS:** 0.8
- **GRL:** A
- **WORD COUNT:** 45

- **CURRICULUM CONNECTIONS:** nature, trees

Skills to Teach

- **HIGH-FREQUENCY WORDS:** have
- **CONTENT WORDS:** bark, branches, flowers, fruit, holes, homes, leaves, needles, nests, nuts, roots, seeds, trees, trunks, twigs
- **PUNCTUATION:** periods
- **WORD STUDY:** irregular plural (*leaves*); initial consonant clusters (*branches, flowers, fruit, trees, trunks, twigs*); long /e/, spelled ee (*needles, seeds, trees*), ea (*leaves*)
- **TEXT TYPE:** information report

Before Reading Activities

- Read the title and give a simple statement of the main idea.
- Have students "walk" through the book and talk about what they see in the pictures.
- Introduce new vocabulary by having students predict the first letter and locate the word in the text.
- Discuss any unfamiliar concepts that are in the text.

After Reading Activities

Ask children to think of how we use trees; for example, they might answer that we use them for shade or to make paper. Write their responses on the board. Then encourage them to think of other animals that might use trees, such as birds, insects, or small mammals. How do these animals use trees? They might respond that the animals use trees for food or to make their homes. Write their answers on the board as well and discuss.

Tadpole Books are published by Jump!, 5357 Penn Avenue South, Minneapolis, MN 55419, www.jumplibrary.com

Copyright ©2018 Jump! International copyright reserved in all countries. No part of this book may be reproduced in any form without written permission from the publisher.

Editorial: Hundred Acre Words, LLC **Designer:** Anna Peterson

Photo Credits: Alamy: Kitchin and Hurst, 3; William Leaman, 14. Getty: Panoramic Images, 2. Shutterstock: apiguide, 9; D and D Photo Sudbury, 13; DR Travel Photo and Video, 12; Gerald A. DeBoer, 15; jakkapan, 1; Kenneth Keifer, 8; Martin Fowler, 11; Matauw, 10; Nadezhda Bolotina, 4–5; Peter Kniez, 6; ukmooney, cover; watin, 7.

Library of Congress Cataloging-in-Publication Data
Names: Mayerling, Tim, author.
Title: I see trees / by Tim Mayerling.
Description: Minneapolis, Minnesota: Jump!, Inc., 2017. | Series: Outdoor explorer | Includes index.
Identifiers: LCCN 2017036930 (print) | LCCN 2017039854 (ebook) | ISBN 9781624967238 (ebook) | ISBN 9781620319499 (hardcover: alk. paper) | ISBN 9781620319505 (pbk.)
Subjects: LCSH: Trees—Juvenile literature.
Classification: LCC QK475.8 (ebook) | LCC QK475.8 .M39 2017 (print) | DDC 582.16—dc23
LC record available at https://lccn.loc.gov/2017036930